TINY

For my wonderful agent, Elizabeth —S.L.-J.
For Anne . . . yes . . . that Anne! —R.W.

Text copyright © 2021 by Sally Lloyd-Jones. Jacket and interior illustrations copyright © 2021 by Rowboat Watkins.
All rights reserved. Published in the United States by Anne Schwartz Books, an imprint of
Random House Children's Books, a division of Penguin Random House LLC, New York.
Anne Schwartz Books and the colophon are trademarks of Penguin Random House LLC.

Visit us on the Web! rhcbooks.com
Educators and librarians, for a variety of teaching tools, visit us at RHTeachersLibrarians.com

Library of Congress Cataloging-in-Publication Data
Names: Lloyd-Jones, Sally, author. | Watkins, Rowboat, illustrator. Title: Tiny Cedric / Sally Lloyd-Jones;
[illustrations by] Rowboat Watkins. Description: First edition. | New York: Anne Schwartz Books, [2021] |
Audience: Ages 4–8. | Audience: Grades K–1. | Summary: "A tiny king rids his palace of everyone
bigger than himself, except for the babies"–Provided by publisher.
Identifiers: LCCN 2020046328 | ISBN 978-1-5247-7072-3 (hardcover) |
ISBN 978-1-5247-7073-0 (lib. bdg.) | ISBN 978-1-5247-7074-7 (ebook)
Subjects: CYAC: Size–Fiction. | Kings, queens, rulers, etc.–Fiction.
Classification: LCC PZ7.L77878 Ti 2021 | DDC [E]–dc23

The text of this book is set in Humana Serif Medium.
The illustrations were rendered on nubby paper with pencil,
graphite, colored pencil, and analog and digital watercolor.
Book design by Martha Rago
MANUFACTURED IN CHINA
10 9 8 7 6 5 4 3 2 1
First Edition

Sally Lloyd-Jones

CEDRIC

Illustrated by **Rowboat Watkins**

a·s·b
anne schwartz books

ONCE UPON A TIME . . .

with the longest name

on the shortest street

with the HUGEST throne

in the biggest palace

sat the tiniest king.

His name was Cedric,
King ME the First.
And he didn't like
being small.

At all.

Every morning,
Tiny Cedric got in his hot-air balloon
and looked down from the sky.
"Everyone's so TEENY!" he cheered.
"I'm all big and tall, and NOT SMALL!"

At breakfast, he enjoyed reading
his newspaper, **The Daily Me.**

He read what he'd done—"How marvelous!" he said.

He read what he'd said—"Oh, I agree!" he laughed.

He saw his photo—"So handsome!" he proclaimed.

But, sometimes, he caught sight of someone bigger, and remembered how small he was.

So Tiny Cedric made a law:

"NO ONE CAN BE TALLER THAN ME!"

This was silly, of course,
because people grow whether
someone likes it or not.

So Tiny Cedric banished
anyone taller than him
from the palace.

Which was everyone.
Basically.

Next, he built a wall.

"Now I won't accidentally see someone big!" he said.

Still, to be extra safe, he bricked
up the windows and put up mirrors.

Special mirrors that made him look GIGANTIC.
Everywhere he looked, he saw himself smiling back at himself.
"I'm all big and tall, and NOT SMALL!" he cheered.
"PERFECT!"

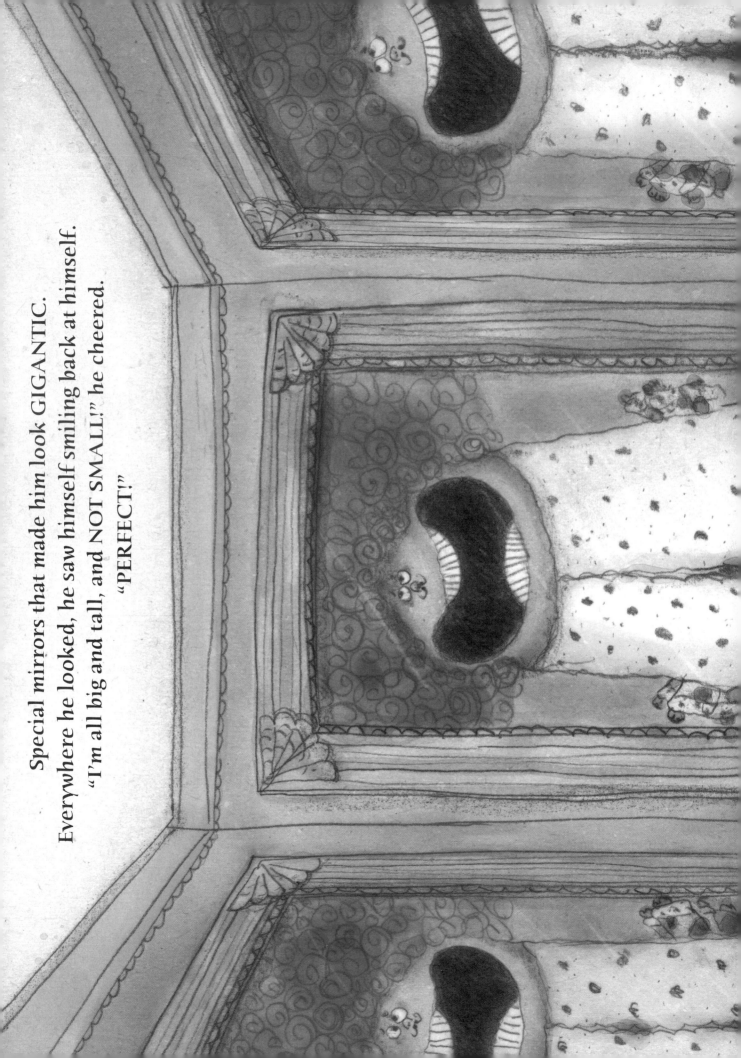

Except it wasn't.

The next morning,
when he came down
for breakfast—
THERE WAS NO
BREAKFAST!

"GET MY
SERVANTS!"
he shouted.

Then he remembered.

He didn't have any.

The only people left in the castle were the babies.

So Tiny Cedric hired them to perform the Royal Duties
and mostly just be smaller than him.

But the baby presiding over meetings fell asleep in her porridge.

The Royal Librarian kept eating the books.

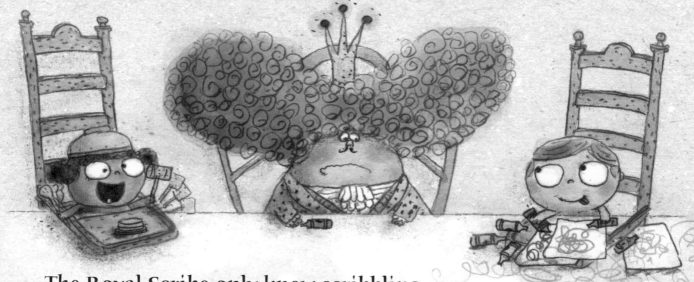

The Royal Scribe only knew scribbling.

The Royal Dresser just
kept undressing herself.

And the Royal Taster ate everything.

It wasn't satisfactory.

When the babies climbed the bookcases and brought them

crashing down on top of the tiny king, it was the last straw.

"HELP!"
he cried
in an
underneath
voice.
"CALL
THE
FIRE
BRIGADE!"

The Baby Fire Brigade arrived immediately.

Unfortunately, they got
tangled up in the hoses and
sprayed water all over his
tiny vestments . . .

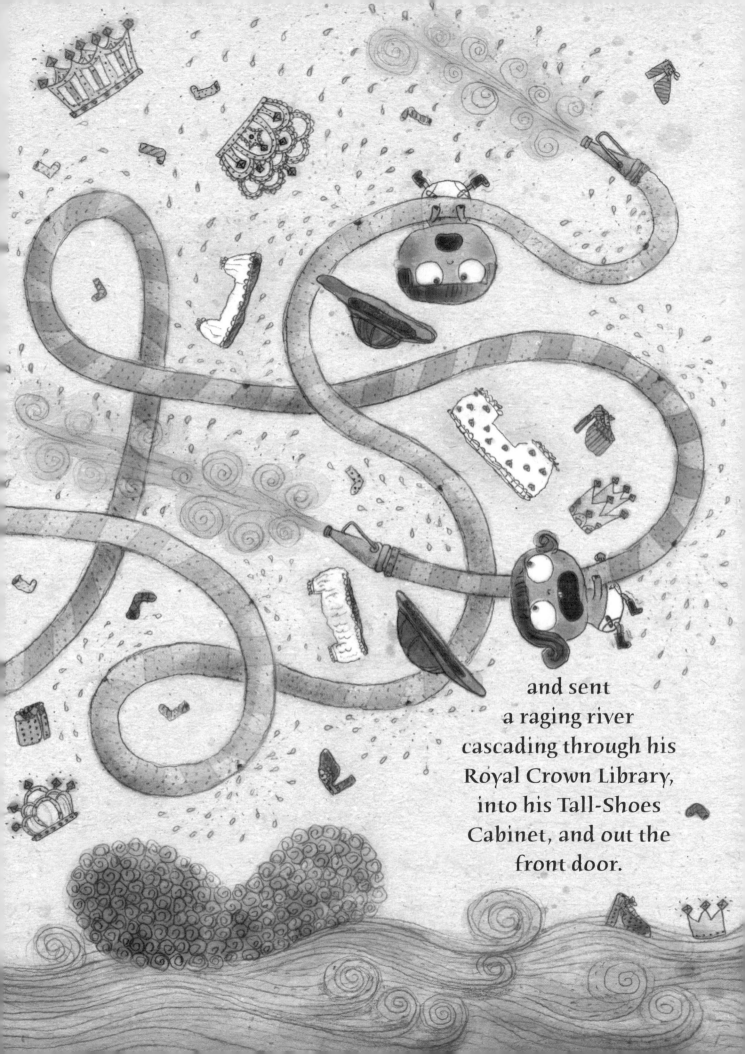

and sent
a raging river
cascading through his
Royal Crown Library,
into his Tall-Shoes
Cabinet, and out the
front door.

That night, the babies
were too scared to go
to sleep, so they slept
in the king's bed.

It wasn't ideal.

The next morning,
everyone woke up
hungry.

But since the Royal Chef only knew sloppymush,
the tiny king had to cook instead.

Then the babies wanted to go on adventures.

But since babies don't know about shoelaces,
the tiny king had to tie everyone's.

By the Royal Duck Pond,
they cried for milk and cookies.

So the tiny king had
to fetch them their snack.

And in the Dandelion Garden,
they fell over and got boo-boos.

So the tiny king had
to kiss them better.

Finally, at nine o'clock, when the babies were too tired, of course the tiny king had to read them their bedtime story.

In the middle of the night, when the babies
woke up all crying for their mommies,
the king cuddled them back to sleep.

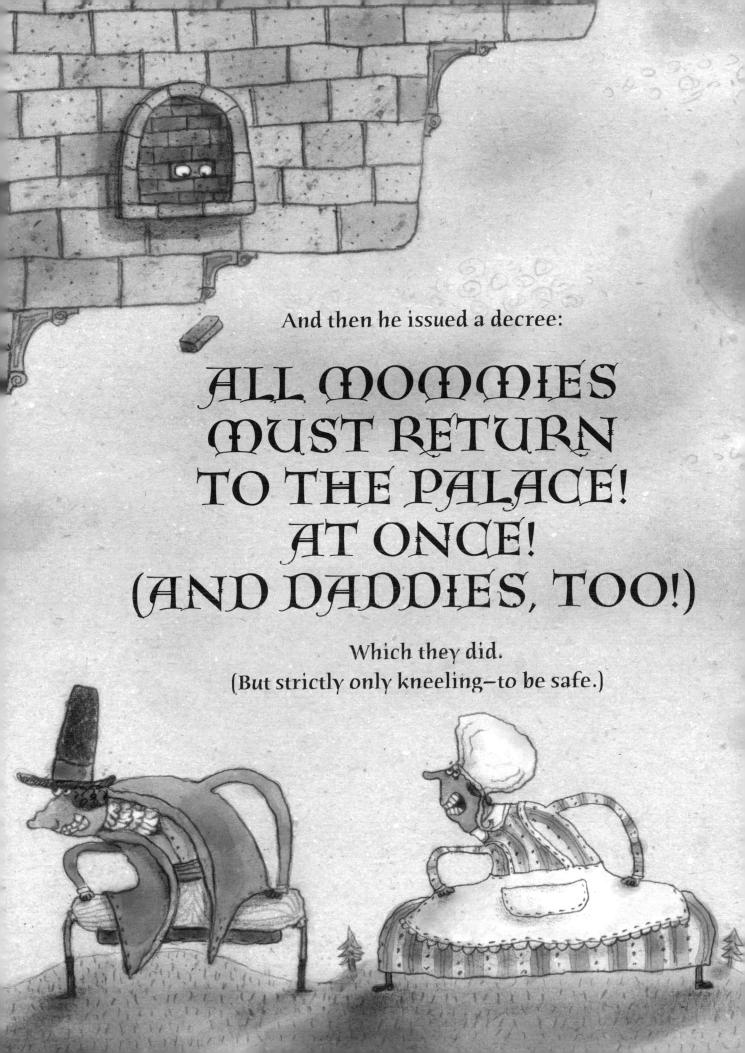

And then he issued a decree:

ALL MOMMIES MUST RETURN TO THE PALACE! AT ONCE! (AND DADDIES, TOO!)

Which they did.
(But strictly only kneeling—to be safe.)

And every day, the babies grew . . .

and grew (as babies do) . . .

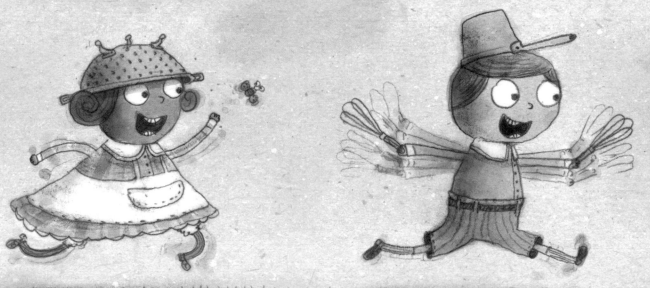

until at last they were bigger than the tiny king.

And do you know what?

Tiny Cedric was far
too happy to even notice.